SHIPWRECKED!

SHIPWRECKED!

AQUATIC ADVENTURES IN THE OVERWORLD

BOOK FIVE

AN UNOFFICIAL MINECRAFTERS NOVEL

MAGGIE MARKS

Sky Pony Press
New York

AQUATIC ADVENTURES IN THE OVERWORLD: SHIPWRECKED!

Copyright © 2020 by Hollan Publishing, Inc.

Minecraft® is a registered trademark of Notch Development AB. The Minecraft game is copyright © Mojang AB.

Sky Pony Press books may be purchased in bulk at special discounts for sales promotion, corporate gifts, fund-raising, or educational purposes. Special editions can also be created to specifications. For details, contact the Special Sales Department, Sky Pony Press, 307 West 36th Street, 11th Floor, New York, NY 10018 or info@skyhorsepublishing.com.

Sky Pony® is a registered trademark of Skyhorse Publishing, Inc.®, a Delaware corporation.

Visit our website at www.skyponypress.com.

10 9 8 7 6 5 4 3 2 1

Library of Congress Cataloging-in-Publication Data is available on file.

Special thanks to Erin L. Falligant.

Cover illustration by Amanda Brack
Cover design by Brian Peterson

Hardcover ISBN: 978-1-5107-5328-0
E-book ISBN: 978-1-5107-5329-7

Printed in the United States of America

TABLE OF CONTENTS

CHAPTER 1

Thwack!

Asher swung at the wooden plank with his axe. As it snapped in two, he lifted the longer piece and handed it to Mason. "How's that?"

Mason took the weathered board from his brother. "Perfect!" He placed it on the stone wall, just above the other four shelves they had made.

He and Asher had been helping Ms. Beacon restore her underwater cave after a fire. She hadn't wanted their help at first. *She didn't trust us,* Mason remembered. *Until we helped her gather more potion ingredients to replace the ones that were lost.*

Now the rebuilt shelves held jars filled with those ingredients, like fermented spider eyes, brown mushrooms, and gunpowder. *And Ms. Beacon and I are sort of, almost, friends,* Mason thought with a smile.

Ms. Beacon crouched beside a low shelf to slide dried Nether wart out of a jar. She screwed the lid back on tightly. Then she drifted back toward the brewing stand, her white robes trailing behind her.

"Are you brewing potion of invisibility?" Asher asked, hope flickering in his green eyes.

"You'll see," said their friend Luna, who stood beside Ms. Beacon's cauldron. "Be patient."

"I've *been* patient, all morning. And now I have a blister." Asher studied his palms. "How much longer do we have to work?"

Mason checked the wall. "Just one more shelf," he said, "and then we'll be done."

Asher's eyes lit up again. He reached for a plank from the stack of wood they'd brought.

The planks were from Uncle Bart's ship, the one that had gone down during a storm. The memory of that storm—and of losing Uncle Bart—still churned in Mason's chest. *But at least the planks are going to good use,* he thought.

Asher swung his pickaxe with a grunt. *Thwack! Crack!* The board split in two.

And so did Asher's axe.

"No!" he cried, studying the handle where the head used to be. "I broke it."

Ms. Beacon hurried over. "So you did," she said. "Maybe we can mend it. Till then, go check my loot chest for another."

Mason and his brother locked eyes. Had Ms. Beacon really given them permission to go into her loot chest?

Asher got there first. As he pried open the lid,

Mason leaned over his brother's shoulder. Gold treasure glowed from deep within the chest: A pile of precious gold nuggets. A rare golden helmet. And a golden apple—the kind Ms. Beacon knew how to use to heal zombie villagers. Asher dug through the chest like a wolf-dog in the dirt.

"Be careful!" Mason hissed in his brother's ear.

"How can I find the pickaxe if I don't touch anything?" Asher protested. He slid aside an enchanted fishing rod and lifted a leather tunic.

"There!" said Mason, pointing. A stone axe peeked out from beneath an enchanted book.

Asher's face drooped. "I was hoping for a gold axe," he whispered. "Or at least iron, like the one I had. But stone? That thing looks heavy as obsidian!"

"A stone axe is better than a broken one," Mason reminded him. He reached for the tool, which did feel heavy. As he lowered it to the ground with a *clunk*, something caught his eye at the bottom of the chest.

Asher saw it too. "What is that?" he asked, leaning forward. "An old robe?"

"I don't know." When Mason touched the tattered gray fabric, he discovered it wasn't fabric at all. It felt leathery, like armor. As he pulled it from the chest, the item slowly slid apart, like a pair of droopy wings.

"Elytra wings!" Asher shouted. When he reached for them, Mason swooped them safely away.

"Don't touch them," he warned. "They're broken. See?" He pointed toward the tattered end of one of the wings.

"We can mend them," said Asher. "Right, Ms. B?"

Mason winced. Asher was the only one who could use the nickname with Ms. Beacon and get away with it. *But does she mind?* Mason wondered.

The old woman raised her lined face from the brewing stand. "Perhaps we can," was all she said.

But Luna shook her head. "There are only three ways to mend Elytra wings," she said. "You have to combine them with another pair of wings in an anvil, or use the mending enchantment, or fight some phantoms for their membranes and mend the wings with those."

Mason shuddered. He'd fought phantoms before, the winged creatures that spawn only when someone hasn't slept for days. *Like after the shipwreck,* he remembered, *when Asher and I were alone on the island.* Mason hadn't slept then. He'd had to stay awake to protect his brother. And the phantoms had spawned and nearly killed them both.

"Do you have another pair of wings?" Asher asked Ms. Beacon.

"No," she said. "Only the one pair."

Asher's shoulders slumped. "Oh."

"But there was an enchanted book in the trunk," Mason remembered. "Does it have the mending enchantment?"

Asher dove back into the trunk, his back side sticking out. "Nope," he called, his voice ringing in the hollow chest. "It's enchanted with feather falling."

Mason studied the items they had pulled from the

chest. "Maybe we can fish for a book enchanted with mending," he said, pointing toward the fishing rod.

Asher groaned. "That'll take way too long! It would be quicker to just fight the phantoms."

Mason shot a sideways look at Ms. Beacon, who wasn't a fan of fighting mobs unless someone was in danger. But she was bottling a potion and didn't seem to hear. She corked the thin bottle of green liquid and handed it to Luna.

Luna held the bottle up to the light of the nearby lava stream. "Forget the Elytra wings," she announced. "We have potion of leaping here. And leaping is the next best thing to flying!"

Asher shot up like a firework rocket. "Can I try it?"

Ms. Beacon nodded. "But just a tad," she warned. "It's very strong."

As Mason reached for the bottle, too, he braced himself for the bitter taste of Nether wart. He squeezed his eyes shut as the potion burned a path down his throat.

Asher was already leaping, taking long, bouncy strides around the cave. "Ha!" he cried. "This is fun!"

Mason took a careful step, hoping he wouldn't hit his head on the ceiling. His legs felt like springs! *Boing, boing, boing* . . . He leaped over the cauldron with a single bound, landing dangerously close to the pool of lava on the far side of the cave.

"Watch out!" called Luna, laughing. She was leaping now too, back and forth from one side of the cave to the other.

Mason jumped upward, away from the lava—just as Asher was coming down. *Smack!* Mason bounced off his brother and hurled toward the stone floor. He braced himself for impact, but felt nothing. He landed on the ground, soft as a feather.

"Are you okay?" Asher called, his face etched with guilt.

"Of course he is," said Luna, leaping over Mason playfully. "Potion of leaping reduces fall damage, too. C'mon!" She reached for Mason's hand and pulled him back up.

When the potion finally wore off, Mason leaned over to catch his breath. "Yep," he said with a grin. "That's almost like flying."

"But flying would be more fun," Asher insisted, gazing at the Elytra wings. "We need to fix those wings. We need a book enchanted with mending!"

Mason caught Luna's eye and shrugged. Once Asher had his mind set on something, there was no stopping him. "I guess we'll be doing some fishing," he said.

Luna grinned. "Good luck with that."

"Here, use this." Ms. Beacon handed him her enchanted fishing rod. "You'll have the luck of the sea," she said with a wink.

As Mason reached for the rod, he felt a flutter of hope in his stomach. *Maybe we* will *catch a book enchanted with mending,* he decided. *Maybe we* will *fix the Elytra wings. And maybe one day soon, we'll be flying!*

* * *

"You've got a bite!" Mason cried.

Asher snapped out of a daydream and grabbed his pole. As he reeled in his catch, his face fell. "Another pufferfish," he said. "Where are all the enchanted books?"

They'd been in the boat for half an hour, and so far, the luck of the sea enchantment hadn't proven so lucky. Their pile of "treasures" swam in a bucket in the back of the boat: two pufferfish and a clownfish.

"We'll find some books," Mason said. "Don't worry."

Asher sighed. "I sure hope so. Because it'll be way more fun to fly over the ocean than it is to row across it."

Mason couldn't argue with that. As he cast his line again, a raindrop plunked off his nose. "Hey, is it supposed to storm?" he asked.

Asher shook his head so hard, the boat rocked beneath them. "No way," he said. "The sky was clear when we came out!"

Mason glanced up. A bank of heavy gray clouds drifted across the extreme hills, heading toward the water.

As the sky darkened, Asher's mood did, too. "Now we're never going to catch an enchanted book," he muttered.

"We can come out again tomorrow," said Mason. "Let's pack up—the water's getting choppy."

He shivered, more with fear than from the cold. Even small storms reminded him of the big one—the one that had taken Uncle Bart away from them. He glanced up again, checking the clouds.

Something else caught his eye in the distance. He blinked twice, wondering if he was imagining it. "Asher." He nudged his brother. "Do you see a ship?" He pointed.

Asher slowly nodded. "I think so," he said, his voice rising.

It had been ages since they'd seen a ship. And this was a big one, too, its sails billowing in the raging wind.

"The storm already caught up to it," said Asher. As the brothers watched, the ship tossed and turned on the rolling waves.

"We'd better get out of here," said Mason, "before it catches up with us!" But his eyes stayed glued to that ship. Because even from this far away, he could tell that the ship was in trouble.

Rain slid sideways in sheets now, stinging his eyes, but he couldn't look away. He reached for his brother's arm, as if holding on to him would somehow keep that ship safe, too.

But it didn't.

The ship began to spin, slowly at first, and then faster. Nausea churned in Mason's stomach. He watched in horror as the ship's stern dipped low amid the waves.

And then the ship disappeared, as if it had never been there at all.

CHAPTER 2

"Where'd it go?" Asher cried, his voice instantly swallowed up by the wind.

Mason couldn't speak. *Down,* he thought with horror. *The ship went down.* He fought the urge to row straight into the storm, to battle the waves in search of survivors.

But he couldn't! The storm was too strong, and the ship was too far away. All Mason could do was get his little brother back to safety—back to the underwater village where they lived. "Row," he called to Asher. "Row!"

Together, they tugged on the oars, paddling toward home. But with every stroke, Mason's mind raced. Who had been on the boat? Had they survived? Were they in the waves now, being sucked downward by the raging water?

That's how our ship sank, he remembered—pulled downward into a bubble column with such force that it had split in two. Uncle Bart had slid right off the deck. *Right in front of me,* thought Mason. He squeezed his eyes shut, trying to block the memory.

There was no time to panic now. He had to get Asher to safety. And he had to get to Luna. Because if there were any survivors from that shipwreck, she would know how to find them. Luna had lived in the underwater village much longer than he and Asher had.

Luna will know what to do, he told himself as he paddled toward home.

*   *   *

"We can't go back out," Luna repeated. "It's still storming out there!" She tapped the glass window of her underwater home.

Mason glanced out, but all he could see was the bright light of the conduit. He and Asher had built it themselves based on the diagram Uncle Bart had sketched in his journal. The turquoise ball spinning in the prismarine base cast a warm glow across the ocean floor.

But up above, the storm still raged. Every few minutes, thunder rumbled. Sea grass slapped against the window as if caught in an angry current.

We're safe down here, thought Mason. *But whoever was sailing on that ship is not.*

"What if there were kids onboard?" he wondered aloud, his voice cracking. "What if they're stranded somewhere, like we were?"

Luna's eyes softened. "I hope not," she said. "But we'll go look—I promise. As soon as it's safe."

"Seventy-two, seventy-three . . ." Asher counted. As thunder shook the glass walls, he ducked. "Yeesh! That sounded like fireworks. But at least the thunder is getting farther apart. The storm is dying down."

Mason nodded. But as the time between thunder claps grew longer, his patience grew shorter. "It's practically over now," he said to Luna. "Can we start looking?"

She chewed her lip and shrugged.

That was all the answer Mason needed. He reached for the potions of water breathing and swiftness that would get them safely to the water's surface.

As he swam down the tunnel of rock that led out of Luna's house, Mason checked to be sure the others were following. Then he shot out of the tunnel, speeding along the coral reef and through the ruins of the underwater village. He barely glanced at Ms. Beacon's cave as they passed. Instead, he kept his eyes trained on the bubble column that would take them up to their rowboat.

Will it still be there? he wondered. *Or will the storm have destroyed that, too?*

When he reached the water's surface, he saw the rowboat bobbing on the waves. He quickly pulled himself over the edge. A couple of inches of water splashed at the bottom of the boat, but it would float. *Yes!* He helped Asher and Luna in and reached for the oars.

"Where to?" asked Luna, searching the cloudy sky.

Mason pointed toward the extreme hills. But his hand wavered. "Wait, was it over there?" he asked Asher.

His brother shrugged. "Everything looks different now," he said.

Luna sighed. "How can we find the ship if we don't even know where to look?" she asked.

Mason swallowed the panic rising in his throat. "We just have to start," he said, "and keep going. Even if it takes all day."

No one argued. But as they raced across the open water, Mason feared what they would find.

Nothing.

The ocean was too vast. And too deep.

After three hours of searching, Luna convinced him to turn around. Or maybe it was his growling stomach. Or the bright sun overhead that now pelted down on them like hot lava.

As they rowed back toward home, Mason sighed. "I wish we could move faster—and cover more ground."

"We could," said Asher, "if we fixed the Elytra wings." His words hung in the air like a lingering potion.

Luna started to protest, but Mason held up his hand. "No, he's right," he said. "That's the only way to search the ocean quickly. We have to search from overhead!"

"But we can't mend the wings!" said Luna. "We already talked about that. There's no way."

Mason swallowed hard. "There's *one* way," he said, meeting Asher's eyes.

Asher's freckled face brightened. "Yep," he said to Luna. "There's one way. We have to fight the phantoms." He actually sounded happy about that.

"You can't stay awake for three days," said Luna.

"Mason did!" Asher reminded her.

"Well, yeah," said Luna. "Because your ship had just wrecked and I hadn't shown up yet to help you." She only half smiled.

Mason's chest tightened at the memory. "Someone else's ship just wrecked," he reminded her. "And they might need our help, too."

Luna licked her lips. "So . . . we're doing this then? We're fighting the phantoms?" Her voice wobbled with the words.

Mason hesitated for just a moment. The last thing he wanted to do was stay awake for three days and fight the winged mobs. But what choice did they have?

Finally, he nodded. "We did it once," he said. "And we can do it again." He only wished he felt half as confident as he sounded.

CHAPTER 3

"**W**e shouldn't *all* stay awake," Luna said. "Only one person should. Then the other two will be rested and ready to fight when the phantoms come."

"I'll stay awake," said Mason.

"Me, too," said Asher.

Mason groaned. "That makes two people staying awake, Asher! Luna said only one of us should, and I've already proven I can do it."

"I can, too." Asher crossed his arms.

"Whatever," said Luna, waving her hand in the air. "I'll sleep, as long as you guys promise to keep the campfire going."

"We will," said Asher. "And I have my flint and steel if it goes out." He patted his canvas sack.

Mason stared at the flickering flames, which lit up the sandy beach in front of them and the wreck of Uncle Bart's ship behind them. The fire would keep hostile mobs from spawning. *At least until that third night,* he thought, *when the phantoms will come.*

He smoothed out the goosebumps on his arms. "We'll keep the fire going," he said.

Asher was already adding another log to the fire pit. As he stoked the flames and Luna unrolled her sleeping mat in the sand, Mason felt a wave of gratitude. At least he wouldn't be fighting the phantoms alone this time.

As night wore on, Asher stayed awake by counting the stars in the sky. "Three hundred sixty-eight, three hundred sixty-nine . . ." He yawned and rested his chin on his knees.

"Go to sleep," said Mason. "I've got this."

Asher shook his head, which was sinking lower and lower. Finally, his eyes closed.

When Asher stretched out on the sand and began to snore, Mason suddenly felt very much alone. He scanned the beach from one end to the other. "It's all you now," he whispered. "Just stay awake—and don't freak out."

He paced circles around the campfire, forward and then backward. He threw another piece of cod on the fire, eating his way back to awake. And when nothing else worked, he waded into the waves and splashed cold water on his face.

Finally, the pink glow of the sun laced the horizon. "I made it!" he whispered, pumping his fist.

"Yeah, you made it," said Luna, sitting up in the sand. "You made it through one night. Two more to go." She yawned and gave him a lopsided smile.

"Right," said Mason, his confidence sinking. "Two more nights to go."

He glanced back at the horizon, hoping the sunshine would give him a boost. At this rate, he was going to need all the help he could get.

*   *   *

As Mason took a swig of water, he fought the urge to splash some of it on Asher's face. His brother was snoring, sleeping on the beach—in the middle of the day!

"I've been awake for two and a half days," said Mason. "And Asher can't even stay awake for one?" He kicked at the sand.

Luna chewed her lip. "I hate to say it," she said, "but it's probably good that Asher is resting. The phantoms may come tonight." She cast a sideways glance at Mason, as if wondering if he was up to the fight.

"Don't remind me," he groaned. He was so tired, he felt like he could barely walk a straight line, let alone fight a hostile mob.

"I'm going to fish down by those rocks," Luna said, pointing. "Want to come?"

Mason shook his head. "I'm going to pace the ship."

Luna cocked her head. "For real?"

He nodded. "It keeps me awake." *And reminds me of why I'm doing this,* he thought to himself.

Being back on Uncle Bart's ship was like stepping back in time to those first few horrible days after the shipwreck. *Someone else might be going through that right now,* thought Mason. But he could find them and help them, if he could only stay awake long enough to fight the phantoms and fix those wings.

Just a few more hours, he told himself. *Till sunset.*

But when he looked up, he couldn't tell what time it was. The sky was hazy gray, and a cluster of clouds had gathered. *Is it going to rain?* he wondered.

"Only a mist," Luna had said this morning. "The kind that helps the fish bite."

The thought of fresh-caught fish made Mason's mouth water. He could *definitely* stay awake for that.

As he climbed through the crack in the ship's hull, which now served as a doorway, he checked for mobs lurking in the shadows. His hand grazed the handle of the trident at his waist. Then he hurried toward the staircase that led up to the deck.

The dark oak deck, which had once been polished and smooth, was an obstacle course now, with planks sticking up every which way. Mason picked his way carefully toward the rail and looked over it. Asher was still snoozing in the sand below. If Mason walked to the other end of the deck, could he see Luna fishing near the rocks, too? Maybe.

As he turned around, a gust of wind nudged him off balance. He looked up at the crooked mast, where a sail had once billowed. Now, Asher's tiny pirate flag flapped wildly, as if warning of things to come.

Mason swallowed hard. *Asher and Luna will be here*

with me tonight, when the phantoms come, he reminded himself.

And then he began to pace.

It was almost a hundred steps from one end of the ship to the other. Mason counted them twice. As he began his third pass, the wind picked up and the sky darkened. Luna's "mist" was threatening to turn into a full-on storm.

He shook his head in disgust. It couldn't rain tonight—it couldn't! The phantoms wouldn't come if Mason were inside the ship. He had to be out in open air. *Even if it's pouring rain,* he thought with a sigh.

The wind howled through the cracked hull below, and something rumbled overhead. *Thunder?* thought Mason. *Already?*

He checked the sky. A shadow flitted past, as if the pirate's flag had torn loose from its mast. But, no—it was still there.

Another shape swooshed low. For just a moment, Mason wondered if bats had been wakened by the storm. Then he realized: these were no bats. These were much more deadly.

With the darkening sky, the phantoms had spawned early.

And Mason was all alone.

CHAPTER 4

Mason dove beneath a deck rail and scanned the sky. How many phantoms were there? Four, maybe five?

The winged mobs circled the mast of the ship, swooping lower and lower with each pass. Their green, glowing eyes fixed on Mason.

He opened his mouth to call for Luna and Asher—and then closed it. There was no time.

Mason grabbed his trident just as the first phantom attacked. It dove, angling its wings for speed.

"No!" cried Mason. He blocked the beast with his trident, knocking it backward.

The phantom growled with anger and then rose back up.

Mason wound back his arm, ready to release his trident like an arrow. But how could he? *It's my only weapon!* he realized, tightening his grip. He had left his bow down by the campfire—and there were four more phantoms circling.

Whoosh! One swooped past, nipping at his ear.

Another dove behind him, so close that Mason felt the rush of cold air. He whirled around, swinging his trident wildly, and hit . . . nothing. Frustration bubbled up inside, drowning out his fear.

"Come and get me!" Mason shouted to the mobs overhead.

And they did. One after another, they attacked.

Thwack! Mason struck the first beast in its skeletal wing. It wobbled backward, red with rage.

Smack! He caught the next phantom's tailfeathers.

But they kept coming.

Mason struck again and again until finally—*finally!*—the first mob fell. Its leathery membrane drifted downward. But when a gust of wind snatched it up, the membrane skipped toward the edge of the deck.

"No!" Mason lunged to grab it. Seconds later, a blow to his shoulder knocked him to his knees. He'd turned his back for only a moment, but it was a moment too long.

Searing pain spread down Mason's arm. As his trident slipped from his fingers, he suddenly couldn't breathe. His heart thudded in his ears, louder than the rain or the growling phantoms closing in.

When the deck seemed to slope beneath him, Mason fell forward.

Other mobs were spawning now in the darkness of

the storm. From where he lay on the wet deck, Mason could see them coming—figures staggering up the stairs. No, they weren't staggering. They were *running*.

Mason squinted to see.

The first mob held a trident. As she raced toward him, her eyes raged, as fierce as the phantoms above. And her dark ponytail slapped side to side.

Luna!

He raised a hand to warn her of the phantoms. But he couldn't speak. And now he couldn't see.

Mason's world suddenly faded to black.

* * *

"It's not enough!" Asher cried.

"Shh!" Luna hissed. "Don't tell him."

The voices swirled around, so close that Mason wondered if they were in his own head. He couldn't open his eyes, and his shoulder throbbed. "What's not enough?" he whispered hoarsely.

"Shh," Luna said again, more gently this time. "Don't try to sit up just yet. Let the healing potion do its job."

Healing potion? Mason didn't remember drinking any. The last thing he remembered was pacing on deck, trying to stay awake. And then . . .

"The phantoms!" he cried, sitting up so fast that the world around him spun. "Are they gone?" He opened his eyes just enough to see. Sunshine streamed down onto the wet deck. The storm had passed.

"They're gone," said Asher with a sigh. "We got 'em."

"Well, we fought off one or two of them," said Luna. "Then the sun came out and killed the rest."

Mason turned slowly toward his brother. "So what's wrong?"

Asher shrugged and looked toward Luna, as if asking for permission to speak. But Luna spoke for him. "The phantoms dropped only three membranes on deck. We need four to fix the Elytra wings."

Mason closed his eyes, letting the words sink in. *No!* He rolled his hands into fists. *No, no, no!* He couldn't stay awake and fight the phantoms all over again. It was over. He'd tried, and he'd failed.

He thought of the other ship—the one that had been tossed in the storm like a turtle shell. What had become of the people on board? Had they slipped over the edge of the deck, like Uncle Bart? Like the phantom membrane that Mason had tried to save?

He suddenly opened his eyes. "There's one more."

"Huh?" Asher scrunched up his forehead.

"Another membrane!" Mason tried to pull himself to his feet, but his legs felt too wobbly. "Down there," he pointed, over the edge of the deck. "One of them fell!"

Asher was already running toward the stairs, with Luna close behind. While they searched, Mason crossed his fingers. *Please let them find it,* he thought over and over again.

Then he heard Asher yelp. "Here! I've got it! We have four!"

Mason smiled and laid his head back on deck. And then, finally, he slept.

*　*　*

Tink, tink, tink!

Luna rose from the black iron anvil and wiped the sweat from her brow. "Okay," she said hesitantly. "I think I'm done." She slid the Elytra wings from the anvil and spread them wide. "Do these look right, Ms. Beacon?"

The old woman slid her fingertips across the wings and smiled. "Yes, indeed," she said. "They haven't been mended in years."

When Asher rushed toward the wings, Mason grabbed the back of his shirt to stop him. "We have to be really careful with them," he reminded his brother. "Because if we break them again, that's it."

"We can just fight more—" Asher started to say.

"No," Mason answered firmly. "We can't fight more phantoms. I won't. So be careful with those wings."

Asher nodded, his cheeks pink. "I just want to try them out. You said yourself that we had to hurry if we wanted to try to find the wrecked ship."

Mason nodded. They'd already lost three days in their search. If any survivors were stranded in a rowboat or on land somewhere, they'd be running out of food and water soon. *If they haven't already,* he thought with a shiver.

"You can try the wings on," Luna told Asher, "but

you can't try them out just yet. You have to be on dry land to do that, and find something tall to jump off of."

Asher scratched his chin. "Like what?" he asked. "Like Uncle Bart's ship?"

Mason groaned. The last place he wanted to go was back to the island.

But Luna nodded. "Yes," she said. "That's perfect! We can practice flying on the island, and then row out toward the extreme hills to look for the wrecked ship."

"We?" asked Mason.

Luna shrugged. "Yeah, I'm coming too. We can take turns with the wings."

Ms. Beacon was still admiring the wings, as if they reminded her of a time long ago.

"Do you want to come, too?" Asher asked her.

She gave a rare chuckle. "No, dear," she said. "But . . . I might have some things to send with you."

As the woman hurried back toward her shelf of potions, Mason caught Asher's eye and grinned. Whatever treasures Ms. Beacon came up with, they were bound to be good. And helpful.

Sure enough, she returned with a corked bottle. "Potion of Leaping" was scrawled across the label in her spidery handwriting. "A good leap is the start to a successful flight," she told Asher as she handed him the bottle.

She went to her shelves one more time, and returned with a jar of gunpowder and a stack of red-and-white–striped paper. "Firework rockets," she said to Mason. "They'll propel you faster through the air. Do you know how to make them?"

A memory formed in Mason's mind of a lazy summer afternoon with his dad, rolling up firework rockets in the garage. "I think so," he said, his heart racing. "Thanks, Ms. Beacon!"

Asher's eyes turned even greener with envy. "Can I help make some?" he asked.

"Sure," said Mason. "You just add a little gunpowder and roll up the rocket, like this. See?"

Asher added way more than a "little" gunpowder. His red and white striped rockets were fat as sea cucumbers by the time he was done. "Mine will be super fast," he said with a grin.

As Mason loaded up a bucket with rockets, he suddenly realized what they were about to do. Soon, they would be flying over the deepest waters of the ocean. With a single pair of paper-thin wings. And a bucket full of explosive rockets.

Flying could be fun, thought Mason. *But it could also be deadly.* As he lifted the bucket, his palms began to sweat.

CHAPTER 5

"**L**ook out!" Mason cried, slapping his hands over his eyes. He couldn't bear to watch Asher crash and burn. *Again.*

His brother careened over the sand in his Elytra wings, wobbling like a wounded phantom. He made it to the water before nose-diving, but only barely. *Splash!*

While Luna rushed into the water to help Asher out, Mason stood on shore, shaking his head. "My turn," he announced as Asher staggered from the waves, his shoulders slumped in defeat.

"Fine," said Asher, tugging the damp wings off his shoulders. "But it's harder than it looks!"

I've got this, thought Mason as he strapped on the wings. "Can I have some of the leaping potion?"

Luna hesitated. "We have to save it for when we really need it," she said. "Like when we're out in the middle of the ocean, trying to take flight off a tiny rowboat."

Mason swallowed hard. "Um, right." He headed toward Uncle Bart's ship, which was the tallest thing on the island. As he mounted the steps toward deck, his heart raced. In only seconds, he'd be flying—like the Ender dragon itself. Would he soar high in the sky? Or would he face-plant, like Asher just had three times in a row?

He headed toward the broken rail, where he could stand on the edge of the deck and look right over. The water was about twenty yards away, with plenty of sand between here and there. And gravel. And two very worried faces peering up at him.

"You can do it!" called Luna, but her eyes didn't look so sure.

"Remember to steer!" added Asher.

Mason nodded, his throat too dry to speak.

He inched his toes over the edge of the deck. *No, take a running start,* he reminded himself. He backed up several feet and squared off his shoulders. Then he ran, his heavy wings wobbling with each step. As he launched into the air, he tried not to look down.

Am I flying? he wondered, his heart thudding in his ears. *Or am I falling?*

His stomach dropped as he realized he was doing *both.* The wings caught air, but he didn't know how to control them. And he was heading straight toward Asher.

"Turn!" called Asher, waving his arm to the right.

"I don't know how!" cried Mason. Any second now, he was going to knock his brother off his feet. So he did the only thing he could think of—he veered his body toward the right, straining against the wings.

Miraculously, he changed course, swooping downward to the right and then back up again. And instead of crashing, he caught more air. *Yes!* Mason wanted to cheer. *I'm doing it!* He could feel the power of the wings as they carried him forward over the surf.

Faster and faster he flew. Each time it felt as if he was about to hit the water, he swooped down and back up, catching one more burst of speed.

At last, his feet skimmed the water, and he slowly— and not very gracefully—landed with a *plunk*. As the cold surf seeped through his clothes, he shivered and glanced back toward shore.

Mason's stomach dropped. Asher and Luna were so far away! *How am I going to swim with these heavy wings?* he wondered.

When he saw Luna climb into the rowboat, he blew out a breath of relief. She and Asher met him halfway toward shore. Before Mason could even climb into the boat, Asher bombarded him with questions. "You flew so far! How'd you do that?" he cried. "Will you teach me?"

Mason nodded, wiping his face dry. "I'll try," he said, his cheeks hot with pride.

Luna carefully folded up the wings in the back of the boat. "You'll be able to go even farther with Ms. Beacon's leaping potion," she reminded him.

"And her firework rockets!" added Asher. His eyes danced at the thought.

As Luna paddled back toward shore, Mason felt tugged in the opposite direction—out toward the extreme hills. *We're almost ready now,* he told himself. *Almost ready to search for that missing ship. But we have to hurry!*

As the sun disappeared behind a cloud, he reached for the second oar and began to paddle.

*   *   *

"Do you see her yet?" asked Asher. He stood on a rocky ledge, shading his eyes against the afternoon sun.

Mason blinked. "No, the sun's too bright."

Luna was out there somewhere, taking her turn with the Elytra wings. Only this time, she wasn't practicing. She was searching.

They had all taken a turn, scanning the waters near the hills for that sunken ship. With the extra boost from the firework rockets, they could fly much faster—and farther.

So far, Mason had found the ruins of an underwater village, its buildings looking like puzzle pieces from the sky above. Asher had seen a swimming dragon that turned out to be a sunken log. And Luna had seen . . . well, nothing. But Mason crossed his fingers hoping that by the time she got back, she would have some news.

He checked the sky again, searching for the bluish-gray Elytra wings or the trail of gunsmoke that

Luna's firework rocket would leave behind. But he saw nothing.

"There she is!" cried Asher, pointing.

Luna wasn't flying back—she was walking, wet and tired, uphill along the rocky path. But the way she kept glancing over her shoulder told Mason that she had information. She had seen *something*.

"What happened?" he asked, jogging downhill to greet her.

"I saw the ship," she said simply. "I tried to fly closer to get a better look, but . . . well, let's just say I didn't do enough swooping." She ran her fingers along the edge of a wing, smoothing out a tiny tear.

Mason shaded his eyes. "Where's the ship?" he asked. "Which way?"

Luna pointed out toward the horizon. "There's a tiny part of the deck still above water."

Something exploded in Mason's chest. "Were there any survivors on deck?"

Luna's face fell. "I didn't see anyone."

"Could they have swam to shore?" he asked, his words tumbling out of his mouth.

She shrugged. "It's *really* far out. We can row out to take a look, but one of us should fly above to lead the way."

"Well what are we waiting for?" cried Asher. He started downhill.

"Wait!" cried Luna. "It's someone else's turn with these things." She struggled to slide the heavy wings off her shoulders.

"Mine!" said Asher.

"Wrong," said Mason. "You went before Luna. It's my turn." As he reached for the wings, excitement tingled up and down his spine.

We found it, he told himself. And in just a short while, he'd be able to check for survivors. *Please, please, please don't let us be too late.*

CHAPTER 6

W*hoosh!*

With the firework rocket hissing and sparking at his side, Mason flew like a blaze in the Nether, zooming high above the world below.

"Ouch!" A spark from the rocket stung Mason's hand, but he couldn't let go. Luna had pointed him in the direction of the sunken ship, and he could see the broken mast now. He was nearly there!

As the ship came into view, Mason sucked in his breath. *Don't look down,* he reminded himself. If he looked down, he might *fly* down, and crash on the deck of the wrecked ship itself. So he could only glance at the wreckage out of the corner of his eye.

The mast had cracked and bowed over, its sail tattered. The deck itself looked intact, with smooth oak planks. But the ship sloped downward toward the waves, which meant that the hull was damaged.

That ship is filled with water, thought Mason. If

there were survivors, wouldn't they be out on deck now, waving at him for help? Nothing stirred below, except the *creak* of the captain's wheel as it spun in a slow circle.

And suddenly, Mason was careening straight toward it.

His stomach clenched as he cranked his body to the left, narrowly missing the deck rail. As he swooped back up, his limbs tingled with relief. Then he saw Luna, waving at him from the rowboat beyond.

"Get back here!" she called. "Before you crash!"

He did, taking care this time not to look down until he was gliding toward the rowboat. Then, with a gentle narrowing of his wings, he skidded to a stop in the water just a paddle's length away from the rowboat.

"You almost wrecked!" said Asher, grinning as if he'd just seen the best show in the Overworld.

"But I didn't," said Mason, flushing with embarrassment. "And I got a good look on deck, too."

"Did you see anyone?" asked Asher.

Mason shook his head. "We have to dive down and explore the hull, in case there's anyone trapped inside."

He could feel Luna staring at him, and he knew exactly what she was thinking. *No one could have survived underwater this long.*

"They could have potion of water breathing," he said quickly, "or helmets enchanted with respiration. There could still be someone down there."

"Or there could be treasure chests," said Asher.

Mason shot him a look. "Is that all you care about?"

Asher shrugged. "If anyone was on the boat, they would have swam to shore by now," he said.

Mason glanced at the hills, which were awfully far away. He wondered if they should row toward shore and start searching there. But the shipwreck called him back with the lonely *creak* of the captain's wheel. *Someone could still be in the hull,* he thought again. *We have to at least look!*

Luna finally agreed. "I'll stay in the rowboat, so that we have a way home," she said. "You two drink some potions and go explore that ship. But be careful!"

Mason left the Elytra wings in the safety of the boat. After quick swigs of potions of water breathing and of night vision, he dove into the waves. He inhaled deeply, letting the water cool his lungs. Then he checked over his shoulder to be sure Asher was coming. A splash of water and flurry of limbs said yes, so Mason gave a swift kick and swam toward the hulking wreckage of the ship.

He could see, even from a distance, the jagged crack in the side of the hull. *That's why the ship sank so fast!* he realized. As a school of tropical fish darted through the crack, Mason followed.

Inside, he let his eyes adjust for a moment. Furniture was strewn this way and that. A chest had been overturned, with maps and stray pieces of paper floating in every direction. Waterlogged books piled into one corner of the room. A compass bobbed in the water, its red arrow pointing down.

Mason picked his way past the floating contents

and started down the hall. As he passed the supply room, he poked his head inside. It was empty, except for a few floating carrots and a sea turtle who had claimed the furnace as his own. Another flooded room held an anvil and a crafting table, a long crack running down its swollen side.

As the hallway narrowed, Mason pushed himself off both sides to gain traction. He was swimming upward now, he could tell. Sunlight filtered down through some crack or window above. And one more doorway remained before the staircase that would lead toward deck.

Mason's heart thudded in his ears. Would someone be inside that last room? *There's only one way to find out,* he thought. He took a strong stroke and made his way into the room.

It had windows—small round portholes that gave glimpses of the blue sky beyond. In the shafts of light that filtered through, Mason scanned the contents of the room. It held nothing but treasure chests, lining all four walls.

Some of the lids were askew, as if the raging waves of the storm had pried them loose to see what was inside. As Mason searched the murky water, he sucked in his breath. Shiny gold ingots, emeralds, and diamonds littered the cabin floor like wildflowers.

He rubbed his eyes, as if dreaming. Was all this real? Could it possibly be?

Before he could take a closer look, someone blew past him. *Asher* had just discovered the treasure, too.

He practically dove into the nearest chest, pulling out handfuls of emeralds.

But as he whirled around to show Mason, Asher froze. His mouth fell open, and he stared past Mason at the doorway beyond.

Something's there, thought Mason, his chest tight. He fumbled for his trident.

The ship had seemed empty, but now he knew.

They were not alone.

CHAPTER 7

Mason spun toward the doorway, ready to face a hostile mob. Instead, he came face to face with . . .

. . . a teenaged girl.

He blew out a breath of relief, until he spotted the expression on her face. Her eyebrows were furrowed, her mouth set in a tight line. She held a glowing trident, raised and ready.

Then someone pushed past her—a younger boy with the same brown hair and brooding eyes. *They're brother and sister,* Mason knew in an instant. *But why are they so angry?*

The boy half-swam, half-strode toward Asher, who was still floating beside the treasure chest. With the edge of his sharp sword, the boy forced down the lid of the chest and waved Asher away.

Asher shot Mason a questioning look.

Just do what he says! Mason wanted to holler. He

swam toward Asher and tugged on his hand, pulling him away from the chest.

The teenaged girl had entered the room now, too. For a moment, no one moved. Mason kept his fingertips on his trident, just in case. And his mind raced. *Are these griefers, come to claim the treasure as their own?* he wondered.

The girl's eyes flickered around the room, as if she were weighing her options. Her brother watched her, waiting, holding his sword firmly in his hand.

When she finally pointed up, toward the deck above, Mason understood. She wanted them out of that room—away from the treasure. *That's okay. It's safer up there,* thought Mason. *We can call out to Luna. And we can dive overboard if we need to.* He urged Asher to follow him out of the room.

Mason swam slowly up the steps after the brunette girl. When they reached the deck, he broke through the surface of the water. Asher's head popped out seconds later. "Are you okay?" Mason asked.

His brother nodded. "Who are they?" he whispered.

"I don't know," said Mason. But suspicions swirled in his mind. *Either this ship—and treasure—belongs to them, or they're griefers here to steal it.*

There was one way to find out. He turned toward the girl. "Was this your ship?" he asked. "Do you need help?"

She didn't respond. She pressed her lips together and studied Mason as if he were some new specimen of fish that had washed ashore.

It's not her ship! he decided. *Which means she and her brother are griefers. Which means . . . Asher and I are in trouble.*

The brown-haired boy gestured toward Mason's trident. "What enchantment do you have?" His voice sounded as sharp as his weapon.

Should I tell him? Mason wondered. *Will he steal it for himself?*

"Riptide," Asher blurted. He puffed out his chest, as if bragging about his brother's enchanted weapon. Then he pointed to his own weapon, an old bow from Uncle Bart's ship. "My bow's not enchanted yet, but the arrows are plenty sharp."

Stop talking! Mason willed him with his eyes.

But Asher was on a roll now. "What is hers enchanted with?" he asked, pointing toward the glowing trident in the girl's hands.

The boy didn't waste any time telling him. "Impaling."

Mason flinched—he couldn't help it. Impaling was the most deadly enchantment a trident could get. It made the weapon *much* more powerful against mobs like guardians and elder guardians. *And maybe against humans, too,* thought Mason, staring at the sharp trident.

The girl holding it stared back, her eyes dark as obsidian.

Hissssss . . .

Mason heard the sound, but he couldn't place it. A memory flashed through his mind of walking through a wooded area, of a green mob stepping out from behind a bush.

"Creeper!" Asher shouted. He grabbed his bow and began loading an arrow.

"Stop!" ordered the girl, holding up her hand.

Something swooped down from the sky, brushing past Mason's shoulder. He dropped to his knees, frozen. Was it a phantom? He instantly covered his head with his hands.

Then he heard Asher cry out—not in pain, but in wonder. "Is that a . . . parrot?"

Mason's head popped up. Sure enough, a lava-red parrot had landed on the teenaged girl's shoulder. It bobbed its head and hissed another greeting.

"Why does it make that sound?" asked Asher, laughing.

"Parrots imitate other mobs," Mason reminded him. "Luna taught us that."

The girl stroked the parrot's head, as if they were best buds. "Hey, Hiss."

"That's so cool," breathed Asher. He took a step forward and held out his hand. "Hi, Hiss!"

The parrot lunged, nipping Asher's finger.

"Hey!" cried Asher, pulling his hand back. A bright bead of blood appeared on his fingertip.

"Hiss doesn't like people," said the girl. Her eyes narrowed, as if to say, *And I don't either.*

Mason's face grew hot with anger. "Well, maybe you could have told us that sooner."

The girl only shrugged.

"Hiss is freaked out because someone was flying around with Elytra wings," said her brother.

Asher, who had been wrapping his wounded finger in his wet shirt, jerked his chin up. "That was us!" he cried. "Me and Mason!"

"Oh, really?" said the girl. She cocked her head and asked a little too sweetly, "Where are those wings now?"

"Don't tell them!" The words came out of Mason's mouth louder than he had intended. Suddenly, three pairs of eyes were on him. "I mean, the wings aren't ours. We gave them back to a friend."

It was half true. The wings belonged to Ms. Beacon, and they had given the wings to Luna to keep safe in the boat. And Luna *was* a friend.

"Where's your 'friend' now?" asked the girl.

Mason silenced Asher with a glance. "Waiting for us. So we need to get going. C'mon, Asher." Then he hesitated, not even sure which way to go. Back down the stairs? Or over the edge of the deck?

The girl made Mason's decision for him. "There's a shortcut back down, over there by the captain's wheel." Her tone of voice made the hair stand up on the back of Mason's neck.

Asher was already looking for the "shortcut." When he took off toward the captain's wheel, Mason had no choice but to follow.

"Where is it?" Asher asked. Seconds later, the planks dropped out from beneath his feet, and he was gone.

"Asher!" Mason raced to the spot, just as the trapdoor slid shut. Panic flooded his chest. Should he go after his brother? Or turn and fight the griefers who had done this to him?

As he whirled around to fight, he saw the sharp tip of a sword, inches from his face. "Don't move," said the boy holding the weapon.

Mason did the only thing he could think of. He rolled backward, through the trap door, and followed Asher down.

He landed with a splash in dark, dank water. As he found his footing, he stood, surprised that the water was only waist deep. But the room was pitch black. "Asher!"

"Here!" cried a voice.

Mason felt his brother's hand on his arm. He grabbed it and held on tight, as if the ground might give way again. "Is there a way out?" he asked, trying to keep his voice steady.

"I don't know," said Asher.

Something flickered in the darkness, blinding Mason for a moment. Then he saw his brother, proudly holding his flint and steel. He lit a torch on the wall and took it in his hand.

As Asher waded around the room, Mason followed. The room had four walls, but no door. If there was a way out, it was hidden. His stomach sunk.

"There's a window!" called Asher. He reached up to wipe the smudged glass with his shirt sleeve. "Do you think I can fit through it?"

Mason studied the porthole. "No," he said. "It's too small." His chest squeezed with fear. How were they going to get out? "Let's see what's in here," he finally said. "Maybe there's an axe. Or TNT." The thought of blowing their way out of the room terrified him, but the thought of staying stuck inside—at the mercy of the griefers—scared him even more.

As he waded across the room, he felt for anything solid beneath the water's surface. When his toe kicked something hard, he knelt down. "It's a chest!"

"A treasure chest?" asked Asher, sounding hopeful.

Mason scoffed. "We don't need treasure right now, Asher," he scolded. "We need an axe."

"Right," said Asher. He dropped down and helped Mason raise the lid. They felt for the contents, pulling them out of the water one by one: A lump of coal. A leather chestplate. And a bow.

But Mason noticed immediately that it wasn't an ordinary bow. It had a heavy wooden handle.

"What is it?" asked Asher, examining the weapon. "Does it shoot arrows?"

Mason nodded. "I think so. It's a crossbow."

Asher blew out his breath. "I'll bet Wither and Wolfie would steal this, if they found it."

"Who?" asked Mason.

"The griefers!" said Asher. "The girl is the tough one, like a Wither boss, and her brother is the tame little wolf that does whatever she asks him to."

Mason laughed out loud. Leave it to Asher to give the griefers nicknames, and such fitting ones, too. The teenaged girl *was* tough as a Wither boss. Mason pictured her enchanted trident and shivered.

"You're right. They'd snatch this crossbow right up," he said, stroking its handle. "But it's not going to help us bust out of this room." As he lowered the weapon, he suddenly remembered something—or someone—who could. *Luna!*

He hurried toward the window and pried it open. The glass pane opened only a crack—definitely not big enough to crawl through, but big enough to holler through. He cupped his hand to his mouth, ready to shout to Luna for help. But the words stuck in his throat.

"I want to call for Luna," he said to Asher, "but it'll put her in danger. She'll come to help us, and she'll run into the griefers."

Asher nodded solemnly.

So Mason shut the window and slumped back down, sitting on the lid of the trunk.

There was no way out. They'd come to the shipwreck looking for trapped survivors. *But now we're the ones who are trapped,* he realized. *We're the ones who need help!*

CHAPTER 8

Asher rubbed the porthole window again, as if he could rub away the darkness that had settled outside. "Why hasn't Luna come for us?"

Mason shrugged, wishing he could silence the questions running through his own mind. *How long have we been trapped down here? Are we ever going to get out? Did the griefers capture Luna, too?*

"Maybe she did come," he said as brightly as he could. "Maybe she looked for us and just couldn't find us. I mean, this is a secret room, right?"

Asher nodded solemnly. "Do you think she went back home?"

"Nah," said Mason, waving his hand. "Luna would never leave us behind We just have to find a way to let her know where we are." *Without the griefers hearing us or hurting her,* he thought but didn't say.

Asher frowned. "Can we send her a secret message?"

Mason nodded. "Maybe. But how?"

Asher shrugged. "We could send smoke signals, like from a campfire!"

Mason glanced around the flooded room. "You want to build a campfire? In here?"

Asher's face fell. "Yeah, maybe not." He sunk down like a deflated pufferfish. "But maybe—"

"Shh!" At the sound of boards creaking above, Mason held his finger to his lips.

Asher cocked his ear toward the trapdoor.

Muffled voices floated above, but Mason could make out only a few words: ". . . food . . . time . . . treasure."

"Are the griefers making dinner plans?" he whispered. "Who could eat at a time like this?"

As if right on cue, Asher's stomach growled. He gave Mason a guilty shrug. "I mean, we *have* been down here a long time."

When the trapdoor above cracked open, Mason's heart skipped a beat. He gripped his trident with one hand and shaded his eyes with the other, looking up through the shadows.

"Luna?" called Asher. "Is that you?"

"No," came the voice of Wolfie, the brown-haired boy. "I'm lowering down dinner. Look out, or you'll get hit on the head."

Seconds later, a bucket dropped, tied to a lead rope. Mason peered inside, afraid of what he might find. *What kind of dinner do griefers serve their victims?* he wondered. *Rotten flesh?* He was surprised to see two steaming-hot potatoes.

Asher reached in so quickly, he burned his fingers. "Ooh . . . hot, hot," he said, shaking his hand before trying again.

Mason carefully took his potato, too. But as the bucket shot back up and the trapdoor lowered, he had a horrible thought. "Don't eat that!"

"Why not?" Asher whined. "I'm starving!"

"Because it could be poisonous!" said Mason. "It would be a quick way for the griefers to get rid of us so they could steal all the treasure."

Asher's potato froze, inches from his mouth. "Nah," he said. "If they wanted us gone, they could just use their weapons on us." Before Mason could stop him, he took a gigantic bite. He waved his hand in front of his mouth to cool it down.

"Asher!" Mason fought the urge to stick his hand in his brother's mouth and pull the potato back out.

Asher shrugged. "A boy's gotta eat." He ate every last bite of potato, and then licked his fingers clean. Then he started eyeing up Mason's potato, too. "You going to eat that?"

Mason hesitated. There was no telling when their next meal was coming. *But there's also no telling how long that potato has been floating in the flooded supply chest,* he thought, his stomach churning.

Suddenly, Asher leaned backward. "I don't feel so well," he said, holding his stomach. In the flickering torchlight, his face had grown pale as a ghast's.

"Are you sick?" asked Mason.

Asher answered by sliding downward in the water.

"No!" said Mason. "You have to stay awake. You can't lie down in here." He gently slapped his brother's cheeks, wondering what Luna would do if she were here. She'd pull out potion of healing, or a bottle of milk, and have Asher back to good in no time.

But Luna's not here, he reminded himself. *It's just me and Asher, trapped by two griefers who want to do us harm.* He knew it with certainty now. And he *had* to get his brother out. He had to find a way to contact Luna!

"Stay awake with me," he said brightly. "Let's come up with a way to send Luna a secret message. It'll be like a game. We can't send smoke signals, but maybe we can use something else, like . . ." His eyes desperately searched the room. "The torch. Can we use the torch?"

Asher's eyes rolled, as if it was all he could do to keep them open.

"What can we light with your flint and steel, Asher?" asked Mason.

Asher's mouth moved, trying to form a word.

"What?" asked Mason. "Say it again, Asher." He held his ear toward his brother's lips.

"Fire . . . works."

Mason shot straight up. "Yes. Yes! Fireworks!"

He propped Asher up against the wall and reached for his canvas sack. "That's brilliant, Asher. If Luna sees a firework rocket, she'll know it's ours, won't she?"

As Asher's eyes started to close, Mason nudged his shoulder. "Should we shoot it out the window? Do you want to use your bow?"

Asher shook his head.

"C'mon, wake up," said Mason, his heart racing. Any moment now, he'd lose his brother to sleep. He couldn't hold him up and fire a rocket into the sky at the same time. He needed Asher to stay awake—just long enough to get Luna's attention.

He scanned the room again, looking for anything that might help. His eyes settled on the weapon resting on the lid of the chest. "Do you want to fire the rocket with the crossbow, Asher?"

Crossbow. The word worked like magic. Asher's eyelids flickered open, and he slowly nodded.

Mason blew out a breath of relief. "Okay, good—that's good. You hold the rocket while I light it, okay?"

As he dug in the sack for the flint and steel, he willed Asher to hold the rocket steady. Carefully, Mason lit the fuse. When the rocket sizzled to life, he placed it in the heavy crossbow.

"Okay, we're aiming now," he said. "Right through the cracked window. Aim high!"

Together, they tilted the heavy crossbow upward. When Mason released the rocket, it sailed through the window, leaving a trail of white smoke behind.

Seconds later, Asher's legs buckled.

Mason lunged, keeping his brother's head above water. "Alright, good work. Luna will see the rocket. She'll come find us."

He helped his brother sit back down on the lid of the chest. As Asher's head fell against Mason's shoulder, Mason watched the fiery rocket fizzle away into darkness.

Then he waited.

But as rain began to fall, his hopes began to fizzle, too.

Because if Luna didn't come soon, it would be too late for Asher.

CHAPTER 9

hump, thump. A noise overhead interrupted Mason's thoughts. "Did you hear that?" he whispered.

Asher didn't respond. His head felt heavy as a cocoa pod on Mason's shoulder.

The griefers, thought Mason, his stomach lurching. *Did they come to finish us off?*

As the trapdoor creaked open, he thought about playing dead. *Maybe if I close my eyes, like Asher, they'll think I ate my potato, too. They'll leave us alone—just take their treasure and go on their merry way.*

He tried, squeezing his eyes shut against the torchlight that flooded the room from above. But someone sucked in her breath.

"Mason! Asher!" she whispered.

He knew that voice. If Asher hadn't been leaning against him, Mason would have jumped for joy. "Luna!"

He opened his eyes and searched the trapdoor above, but he couldn't see Luna at all. The torchlight seemed to bob in thin air, as if hanging from an invisible rope. "Luna? Wh-where are you?"

"Potion of invisibility," she whispered. "I don't want the griefers to see me. Are you okay?"

Mason fought back a wave of emotion. "Asher's not," he whispered. "They poisoned him!" A second thought followed the first. "Are the griefers up there? Luna, look out—they're dangerous!"

"They're gone now, I think," she said. "But be quiet, just in case." Her backpack appeared from out of nowhere. It unzipped itself, and a bottle of potion floated out.

"Give Asher this," she said. "Splash potion of healing." She lowered the potion in the bucket that the griefers left behind.

When the bucket was close enough to reach, Mason fumbled inside for the potion. He uncorked it and dribbled a few drops on Asher's forehead, the way he had seen Luna do before.

He hoped Asher's eyes would flutter right open. That he'd sit up, grin, and say, "What did I miss?"

But he didn't.

In the minute that followed, Mason could hear his own heart thudding in his ears. "Is it too late?" he whispered to Luna.

He could see her dark ponytail now and the top of her face, her worried eyes peering down at Asher's pale face. "No," she said. "Just give the potion time to work."

Slowly—much too slowly—Asher's eyelids began to twitch. He yawned, as if coming out of a deep sleep, and he stammered as he spoke. "D-did you fire the r-rocket?" he asked.

Mason laughed out loud. "*We* fired the rocket. And Luna saw it. She's here now, Asher. You're going to be okay."

Asher smiled, but he kept his eyes closed.

Then realization struck. "How are we going to get him out of here?" asked Mason, looking up at Luna. "It's not like you can raise us up in that bucket!"

Luna's face was clearly visible now. She furrowed her eyebrows. "What can we use from the room? Is there any furniture you can stack?"

Mason thought of the chest they were sitting on. If they turned it on its side, it would be taller—but not tall enough. He shook his head. "We have a chest, some armor, and a crossbow. Oh, and a lump of coal." He sighed.

Luna chewed her lip. "Do you still have your weapons?"

Mason nodded. His trident was strapped to his side, and Asher's bow was slung across his brother's shoulder. "We also found a crossbow."

Luna glanced skyward for a moment, as if searching for inspiration. "Riptide," she finally said. "We'll have to use your riptide."

Mason touched his trident. "You mean my enchanted trident? But . . . riptide only works underwater."

Luna held up her hand. "It's raining out," she said. "So it's worth a try, right?"

Mason swallowed hard. "I'll have to bring Asher with me," he said. "He's heavy."

Luna nodded. "I know, but . . ." she shrugged weakly. "Do you have a better idea?"

Mason shook his head and sighed. "Can you sit on your own, Asher?" he asked, sliding his brother upright.

Asher nodded, and finally opened his eyes.

"Good, because you're going to take a ride—a piggyback ride. Can you hold on tight?"

Mason was surprised when Asher climbed right on, no questions asked. He rested his head on Mason's shoulder, but his grip around Mason's waist felt strong.

"It's now or never," Mason whispered, reaching for his trident. "Stand back, Luna."

She was already gone, the trapdoor clear.

Mason aimed carefully, not wanting to hit the ceiling. He wound back his arm and released, hoping that Luna's plan would work. Seconds later, he felt his body lurch upward, taking Asher with him.

They shot through the trapdoor straight up into the rain. For a moment, Mason wondered if they'd sail right over the captain's wheel. But as the trident turned downward, back toward deck, Mason felt his body tugged downward, too.

Uh-oh. He bent his knees to brace for the fall.

Asher yelped from behind, sounding very much awake. "What's going on?"

"Hang on!" said Mason.

Together, they hit the deck—hard. In the slippery rainwater, Mason's feet skidded from beneath him. He knocked over the bucket tied to the rope and landed on his brother with a *thud*.

"Hey, get off!" said Asher.

Mason rolled over, flexing his fingers and toes to be sure nothing was broken. "Are you okay?" he asked.

Asher nodded, looking much more like his old self. He wiped his face dry and glanced around. "Where are the griefers?"

"Shh!" said Mason. But he scanned the shadows, too, feeling as if danger was very nearby.

"Let's get out of here," said Luna. "I anchored the rowboat down below. All we have to do is jump."

"Wait!" cried Asher. "What about the crossbow?" He pointed down through the trapdoor.

Mason sighed. "There's no time, Asher!"

But Luna shook her head. "He's right. It's a valuable weapon. Let's lower him down with this bucket so he can grab it."

Together, Mason and Luna held tight to the lead rope of the bucket as Asher inched his way back down through the trapdoor. When they hoisted him back up, he proudly held the crossbow. "Alright," he said, strapping the second weapon to his waist. "Now we can go!"

Mason reached for his weapon, which had landed

prongs down in the wooden deck. As he pried the trident loose, he heard the sound.

Hissss . . .

Goosebumps sprang up on Mason's arms. "Look out!" he called, raising his trident for battle.

A few feet away, Asher spun in a circle. "Where is it?" he cried. "Where's the creeper?"

"Here." Luna sounded calm, as if she had just spotted a brown mushroom growing in a patch of weeds.

Mason glanced her way, expecting to come face to face with a hissing green mob. Instead, he saw the flash of wings—red wings. A parrot landed on the rail beside Luna and bobbed his head up and down.

"Don't touch him!" Asher cried. "He'll bite you!"

Luna just smiled. She took a step toward the parrot.

"Stop, Luna," said Mason. "Asher's right! Hiss is dangerous. He belongs to the griefers. *And if he's here,* thought Mason, *the griefers must be, too!* His chest tightened as he scanned the deck again.

Luna stood beside the bird now. She didn't raise her hand. She whispered two simple words: "Hiss, *sit*."

The parrot instantly lowered its tail feathers. Then it hopped back up, flapped its wings, and landed . . .

. . . on Luna's shoulder.

"Hey!" cried Asher. "How'd you do that?"

Luna grinned. "It's just a sweet little bird," she said. "It's nothing to be afraid of." She slowly reached out her hand and stroked the bird's feathers.

Mason shook his head. Leave it to Luna to befriend

the nastiest bird in the Overworld. He was about to congratulate her when a voice rang out in the darkness.

"Put that bird down!"

Fear pricked the back of Mason's neck. Ever so slowly, he glanced over the rail, down at the water below.

Luna's rowboat waited there, but it wasn't empty. Two figures sat in the darkness. *Wither and Wolfie,* thought Mason. Only this time, the nicknames didn't make him smile.

Wolfie held a pair of Elytra wings. *Our wings!* Mason realized with a start. *Is he going to steal them?*

As his eyes flickered back to Wither, Mason sucked in his breath. The girl held her sharp trident poised and ready—the trident enchanted with impaling.

And it was pointed directly at Luna.

CHAPTER 10

"**I** said, put down the bird!" Wither ordered from below, her voice rumbling like thunder.

Luna cleared her throat. "Or . . . what?" She sounded so calm, but from where Mason was standing, he could see her arms shaking.

"Or. I'll. Use. This." Wither jabbed her trident forward, punctuating each word. "That parrot belongs to me."

Luna slowly raised her hand, as if she were going to nudge the bird from her shoulder. Instead, she stroked its head.

What's she doing? Mason wondered. His knees felt weak.

"But if you throw your trident at me," said Luna in a low, steady voice, "you might hurt your bird."

In the silence that followed, Mason blew out his breath. Luna was right—there was no way Wither would throw her trident at Luna if Hiss was anywhere nearby.

When Wither spoke again, her voice was cold as ice. "Then we'll take your Elytra wings instead."

Asher sprinted toward the rail. "No!" he said. "If you take our wings, we'll take your parrot!"

"Then we'll break your wings!" shouted Wolfie. He stood, holding the wings in his hands as if he could twist and destroy them at any second.

"Sit down!" snapped his sister as the boat began to rock.

He did. But he kept his eyes trained on Asher, and Asher wouldn't take his eyes off those wings.

For a few moments, no one moved. Mason studied Luna's face, wondering if she had a plan. Luna *always* had a plan. She opened her mouth, as if to speak, just as a crack of lightning lit up the sky.

The parrot squawked. And flapped its wings. And took off.

Luna froze. Then she hit the deck, out of range of the griefer's trident, and reached for her own. "Get ready!" she shouted to Mason.

As he gripped his trident, he wondered. *Would the griefers really attack?*

He suddenly pictured Asher's pale face. They *had* already attacked. They had poisoned Asher with that potato! So what would stop them from doing more damage now?

"Asher, get down!" Mason cried, tugging his brother away from the rail.

But Asher's eyes were glued to the boat below. He raised his hand, pointing.

When Mason looked again, he saw that the boat was on the move. The griefers weren't fighting. They were *leaving*, taking the Elytra wings with them—and the rowboat.

"That's our way home," Luna cried, jumping to her feet. "We have to go after them!"

Asher was already climbing the rail, ready to dive into the water.

"Asher, wait!" cried Mason. "We need a plan."

"He's right," said Luna, catching her breath. "We can't fight them from the water. We'd be easy targets."

"We've got to get *into* the boat," said Mason, pacing alongside the rail. He suddenly stopped. "I could launch my trident. The riptide enchantment would take me with it, straight into the boat!" His heart raced at the thought.

Luna shook her head. "Riptide won't work," she said. "It stopped raining." She held up a palm, as if to prove her point. "We can't get into the boat. But maybe we can find a way to stop it—a way to pull it backward."

"Like with a rope?" asked Asher. He pointed at the bucket resting beside the open trapdoor. The long lead rope tied to the bucket fell in a tangled heap on deck.

Luna blew out her breath. "Asher, you're a genius!" She ran toward the bucket and began untying the rope. "Help me, guys!"

Moments later, they had tied one end of the rope to the bottom of the ship's mast, and the other end to the arrow poised in Asher's crossbow. Together, Mason and Asher steadied the crossbow on the deck rail.

"Hurry!" said Luna. "And make sure you aim low—for the boat."

Mason squeezed his eyes shut, not wanting to picture what would happen if they aimed too high. *Maybe the griefers can attack humans,* he thought. *But can I?*

"On the count of the three," he said to Asher, opening his eyes wide. Together, they pulled back the arrow . . . and released.

It shot through the air like lightning. Instantly, the piled rope behind the brothers began unraveling, whirring round and round until only a few coils remained. *Please let it be long enough!* thought Mason, crossing his fingers.

Thwack! He heard the arrow make contact with the wooden hull of the boat.

Snap! The rope ran out, stretching taught between the mast and the rowboat.

"Did it work?" Asher whispered into the darkness.

The yelp of the griefers in the distance said that it had.

"Help me pull!" cried Luna as she tugged on the rope, pulling the boat back toward the ship.

Using the deck rail like a lever, the three of them pulled, hand over hand. Soon, Mason's palms burned. "What if they jump out?" he asked Luna.

She gritted her teeth, straining with each tug on the rope. "We'll . . . still . . . have . . . the boat!"

Right, thought Mason. He tugged harder.

But when the boat came back into view, it wasn't empty. The griefers were still on board. And this time, both of their weapons were raised. "What do you want?" Wither cried out, her voice thick with anger.

"We want our wings," Asher retorted. "Give them back!"

"Why?" asked her brother. "What do you need them for?"

This time, Mason answered first. "We were using the wings to try to find someone," he said. "To find the people who went down with this ship. We were trying to *help* them!" *Unlike you,* he thought angrily, *who only want to hurt people. Who only want to steal from them!*

Slowly, Wither sat down in the boat. She lowered her weapon. For a long moment or two, she said nothing. Then she finally spoke. "You were trying to find *us,*" she said.

Huh? Mason glanced sideways at Luna, who looked just as confused as he felt.

Wither continued. "We're the ones who went down with this ship."

Mason wanted to argue. He opened his mouth and then closed it. Could what the girl was saying be true?

CHAPTER 11

"**T**his isn't your ship," countered Asher. "You just want the treasure!"

Luna touched his arm to quiet him, but doubts raced through Mason's mind, too. "I asked you once before if this was your boat," he called to Wither over the deck rail. "Why didn't you say yes?"

She said nothing, but Wolfie's voice rang out through the darkness. "Because our parents told us not to!"

Parents? Mason whirled around, half expecting to see them standing on deck. Was there someone else on board this ship?

"They're not here," Wither said quickly. "They were in a rowboat fixing the cracked hull when the storm rolled in. But we've learned from our parents to trust *no one.*"

Probably because they're treasure hunters, thought Mason, picturing the room below deck filled with treasure chests. He felt another rush of anger. "So you pushed us through a trapdoor?" he blurted. "You were just going to leave us down there?"

Wither's face hardened. "We thought you were griefers, here to steal our parents' treasure."

"*You're* the griefers!" said Asher, his cheeks flaming red.

Mason thought of how pale his brother had been just a short while earlier. "You're *worse* than griefers," he said, his voice exploding. "You poisoned my brother with those potatoes!"

Wither whirled around to face Wolfie. "You fed them those old potatoes?"

He slunk backward like a guilty dog. "I . . . I th-thought they'd be hungry," he stammered.

Mason slowly blew out his breath. He turned to face Luna, a question in his eyes. *Do you believe them?*

Her face softened, which meant she did. *But do I?* Mason wondered. He wasn't so sure. "Where are your parents now?" he asked.

Wither shrugged ever so slightly. "Nearby," she said simply.

But as choppy waves battered the sunken hull below, Mason felt a niggle of doubt. Whoever her parents were—treasure hunters, or worse yet, griefers who had stolen that treasure from someone else—they weren't here now. Which meant that maybe they'd been lost in the storm.

"We're coming back on board," Wither announced, tugging on the rope until the boat drifted closer.

But as it came clearly into view, Asher pointed at

the back of the boat. "Wait . . ." he said. "If you're not griefers, why did you steal our Elytra wings?"

The hair on the back of Mason's neck prickled. Asher was right—they *had* taken the wings.

"Because our wings are broken!" insisted Wolfie. "We need them to find our parents."

"So give ours back and fix your own," Asher snapped. "Luna knows how."

Luna flashed him a look. "I can't," she said quickly. "Not without an anvil and the mending enchantment."

Wither had pulled the rowboat so close now, Mason could see her eyes flashing. "We have an anvil," she said. "And plenty of enchanted books. Fix our wings, and we'll give yours back."

Asher reached for the deck rail, as if he were about to leap over the deck rail and *take* the wings back. Mason grabbed the back of his shirt. "Okay," he said quickly. "We'll fix your wings—if we can."

"We?" said Luna sharply.

"I'll help you," he said under his breath. "It's better than fighting them for our Elytra, right?"

Luna glanced back at Wither—and the sharp trident in her hands. "Fine," said Luna. "But as soon as they're fixed, we're taking ours and going home."

Wither nodded. "We'll wait here," she said. She patted the edge of the boat, as if to say, *If you don't come through, we'll steal your rowboat.*

"C'mon," Mason said, before Luna could change her mind. "We have an enchanted book to find."

"I don't think so," said Luna. "You and Asher find

the anvil and the book. I'm going to keep an eye on our friends."

If Luna had trusted the siblings a moment ago, she didn't seem to now. So Mason left here there, leaning against the rail with her trident, her eyes dark and brooding.

We have to hurry, he thought as he led Asher down the deck stairs. A storm was brewing, and this time, it had nothing to do with thunder and lightning.

*   *   *

Flame enchantment.

Fire protection.

Aqua affinity.

The stack of books on the treasure chest was growing taller, but still, he and Asher hadn't found the mending enchantment.

Mason swam back to the corner of the water-logged room for one more look. He dove low and grabbed two more slippery books from the bottom of the wrecked ship. He quickly checked their enchantments.

Blast protection and *luck of the sea.*

He tossed them toward the chest and balled his hands into fists. *We have to find the mending enchantment!* he wanted to shout. *If we don't, how will we ever leave this ship? How will we get home?*

As a haze of darkness fell over the room, Mason's pulse quickened. The potion of night vision he'd taken was fading, which meant his potion of water breathing would soon fade, too.

He tapped Asher on the shoulder and pointed upward, but Asher shook his head. He pointed toward his turtle shell helmet, which meant he'd be alright underwater for a bit longer.

Mason quickly made his way down the long, dark hall. The farther he swam, the *faster* he swam. Dread was forming in his gut now.

As soon as he surfaced back on deck, Luna's head whirled around, her eyes hopeful.

He shook his head. "We didn't find it. Not yet." He reached for her backpack to get more potions, and chanced a glance over the rail to be sure the rowboat was still there.

Wither stared directly back at him. From the boat behind, Wolfie began to whistle.

They're up to something, Mason thought. *But what?*

Before he could investigate, someone hollered.

"I found it!" Asher cried. "The mending enchantment!" He waved a warped, dripping-wet book in his hands.

Relief flooded Mason's chest. "Good work, Asher!" he called.

In just a short while, they'd be able to mend the broken wings. But would it be enough?

He glanced again at the siblings in the boat below. *When the wings are mended, will they give us back our boat?* he wondered.

As the whistling started up again, he wasn't so sure.

* * *

As Mason watched the rowboat bob in the waves, his eyelids grew heavy. *Stay awake!* he scolded himself. *It won't be much longer now.*

Luna and Asher had found the broken wings in the treasure room, right where Wither had said they would be. Luna was mending the wings below deck, using the old black anvil. So what was taking so long?

Mason pinched his cheek, hoping the pain would wake him up. He glanced again at the boat below. Wither slid sideways, as if resting. Behind her, Mason could see only a glimpse of Wolfie's head, leaning over the edge of the boat. He had something shiny in his hands—a pickaxe? And he was slowly sawing at something, back and forth.

The rope!

"Stop!" Mason shouted.

Wolfie froze, his pickaxe in midair. But his sister— who wasn't sleeping at all—murmured something, and he started sawing again.

Mason could see the first few strands of rope starting to fray. Any moment now, the rope would snap. He drew his trident and aimed at the boat below. *But will I really use it?* he wondered. *Could I?*

Snap! The rope gave way. And suddenly, the boat was floating free.

CHAPTER 12

"Stop!" Mason called again as Wither grabbed the oars. A smug smile spread across her face.

"What's happening?" Luna appeared with the mended wings, water drip, drip, dripping to the deck below.

"They're getting away!" Mason cried.

Luna raced toward the edge of the boat. "Wait! I have your wings," she called. "We can make the trade now."

Wolfie gathered up the Elytra wings, as if he was ready to make the trade. But Wither held up her hand.

"We already have wings," she said in an icy voice, "and we have your boat."

Mason's stomach clenched. *We were right not to trust her,* he realized. *She's going to take our boat anyway!*

He turned toward Luna, desperate for her to have a plan. But she sighed, so deeply he thought she was going to sink to the deck itself.

"Why should we trade?" Wither asked again.

"Because we have firework rockets," Asher piped up suddenly. "A sack full of them. And you can't fly very far without rockets." He pulled one out of his backpack and waved it in the air.

That's it! thought Mason, fighting the urge to plant a wet kiss on his brother's cheek.

Wolfie looked so longingly at those rockets, Mason thought he'd fall overboard. But Wither only narrowed her eyes. "Have you flown with those rockets?" she asked.

Asher nodded. "Lots of times—and really far, too. It's how we found your ship."

Mason saw something flicker across the girl's face. "Alright. We'll take your rockets," she said. "And give you back your boat."

She sounds like a farmer making a trade at market, thought Mason, irritation rising in his chest. But at least this time, she seemed to be making good on her deal. She reached for the rope ladder that fell from the side of the boat.

"Wait!" called her brother. "Take these!"

She reached down and carefully grabbed the Elytra wings with one hand. Then she climbed, rung by rung, her trident bouncing at her side.

Luna waited at the top, her own weapon drawn. But Wither barely seemed to notice. She handed Luna the wings and slid easily over the rail. "Let me see," she said to Asher, holding out her hand for a rocket.

He pulled it away, hiding it behind his back.

A shadow fell over Wither's face. Her eyes narrowed again to slits.

"Asher," said Mason, "you made a deal. Give her the rockets." He held his breath.

Asher didn't move. "I don't want to give her all of them. We need some to fly home."

"No, we don't. We can take the boat," said Mason, his voice rising.

But Wither seemed to have a different plan. "Why don't you fly with me?" she said to Asher, her voice suddenly sweet. "Then we can *both* use the rockets."

"No!" Mason said instantly. "He's not going with you."

"He's not," echoed Wolfie, who had just climbed over the rail. "I am!"

Wither ignored him, her eyes still locked with Asher's. "You could help me search—me and Hiss. Did you know that parrots like to fly with you when you're wearing Elytra wings?"

Mason's throat tightened. What game was this girl playing? *At least Asher doesn't like that parrot,* he thought. *He won't want to fly anywhere near it.*

To Mason's surprise, Asher's eyes lit up. "Hiss would fly with me?"

"Sure," said Wither. "I mean, as long as you're flying with me. Want to try it?"

Asher nodded.

"No!" Mason said again. But he saw the flash of determination in Asher's eyes. When his brother set his mind to something, he followed through—even if it meant flying straight into danger.

"Good," said Wither. "We'll wait till Hiss comes back, and then we'll take your rockets and go."

"Hey!" said Wolfie. "What about me?"

"You'll go next," she said to him. "I'll figure out how to use the rockets, and then I can teach you."

He nodded, satisfied. But as Wither began calling for her parrot, Mason shot Luna a look. "What now?" he whispered.

She glanced over the rail at the rowboat below. "We grab Asher and make a break for it?" she half-joked, but her eyes were heavy with worry.

Asher stood beside Wither now as if they were best buds. "Hiss!" he called, searching the sky for that red bird.

It's as if he's totally forgotten how Wither—and her parrot—hurt him! thought Mason. *But I haven't.*

As the sky began to lighten, Asher cupped his hand to his mouth. "Hiss!" he called, again and again.

While Asher searched the skies, Mason quietly lifted his brother's backpack from the deck. He pulled out the firework rockets, one by one, along with the flint and steel.

Luna glanced his way. At first, her eyes held a question. Then she nodded, as if to say, *Yes. Go.* She reached into her own sack and handed him a glass bottle filled with green liquid. "Potion of leaping," she mouthed.

He carefully placed the bottle on the deck at his

feet. Then he slid on the Elytra wings, which were still damp from the rain.

The parrot appeared just as dawn broke. When it swooped past the tattered sail to land on Wither's shoulder, Mason was ready. "Here," he said, handing her the mended wings. "I'm going with you."

"No!" cried Asher.

But Mason was already striking the flint against the steel. When it sparked, he lit the end of a rocket in his hand. Then he handed the flint and steel to Wither, who had quickly slid on her own wings. "Light the rocket, and hold on tight."

Before he could lose his nerve, Mason reached for the potion of leaping. But there was no time. As Asher lunged for the wings, Mason stuffed the potion in his sack. Then he climbed the deck rail and jumped.

The rocket in his hand ignited, shooting him forward. He plunged low, nearly clipping his wing against the rowboat. *Steer!* he reminded himself. He swooped down and then back up, finding a burst of speed.

As he shot out across the ocean waves, he glanced over his shoulder. Wither was close behind, wobbling in her newly mended wings. And back on deck, Asher was hollering, his face beet red. "Come back!" Mason heard him call.

I will, he promised his brother. *Once I know you're safe.*

Then, with another swoop, he led Wither farther away from the boat. Farther away from Asher.

*   *   *

Mason checked the rocket in his hand. It wouldn't last much longer. How far was Wither going to fly?

She was ahead of him now, which is how Mason wanted it. *I need to keep an eye on her,* he decided.

But as he glanced over his shoulder, he saw that Hiss was right behind him. The parrot was close enough to nip Mason's feet. *So who's keeping an eye on whom?* Mason wondered.

At least he had gotten Wither away from his little brother. *Asher's no longer in danger,* he decided. *But . . . I still am.* Behind them, the ship was only a dot on the horizon. And as he glanced right, he saw that the extreme hills were equally far away. Where would they land if they needed to?

"We have to light more rockets!" Mason shouted, wondering if Wither could hear him over the rippling wind.

She turned back only briefly and shook her head no.

Mason's heart raced. He had the rockets, but she had the flint and steel. He couldn't light his own rockets without that!

Can I catch up to her? he wondered. He swooped, dipping low and then back up, using each burst of speed to close the gap between him and Wither. But when she saw him coming, she shot ahead—as if she thought he was chasing her.

"Stop!" he cried. "We need to light more rockets!"

He dipped again, willing the rocket in his hand to take him farther and faster. But as he glanced down, he saw that the rocket was burning up. The trail of white stars shooting out the end had slowed to a trickle. With one last spark, the rocket sizzled . . . and then fell silent.

Mason fell, too, instantly feeling the loss of power. *You can still glide,* he reminded himself. *Don't freak out!*

He held the wings steady, trying not to panic. He glanced desperately up at Wither, who was flying above him. She didn't seem at all concerned about him—or about the rocket that was now sputtering in her own hand.

So Mason veered right, leaving her behind and gliding toward the extreme hills. *She can do what she wants,* he decided. *I have to find land. I have to try!*

It took all his strength to steer the wings now. *Dip, rise, glide. Dip, rise, glide.* He talked himself through the steps, but with each dip, the wings glided a little lower. And the hills still seemed so far away!

He scoped out the nearest strip of land—a small wooded island. He smelled smoke, and then saw a thin column of it rising from the shoreline below.

His wings wobbled, and soon the island was racing up to greet him. Beneath the column of smoke, he could see flickering flames. And he was heading straight toward them.

No! With one last burst of strength, Mason swooped right. The wings responded, carrying him on a gust of wind away from the shore and toward the woods beyond.

He dipped and rose again, over a thick strip of trees—*almost* over the trees. A branch came from nowhere, like a gnarly hand rising up to snatch him. It caught his foot and yanked him backward. Then, in a flurry of twisted wings and tree limbs . . .

. . . he crashed.

CHAPTER 13

Squawk!

Something heavy was resting on Mason's chest. He stretched, as if coming out of a deep sleep—and instantly yelped in pain. "My ankle!"

As he lifted his head, he came face to face with two beady eyes. A sharp black beak. And a red plume of feathers. "Hiss!"

As if on command, the parrot let out a long, slow *hisssss.*

Mason froze, a thousand questions flooding his mind. *Where am I? How long have I been asleep? What happened to my ankle? And will this bird bite off my nose if I move?*

He stared into those beady eyes for what felt like an eternity, until Hiss finally hopped off and started grooming its feathers. Mason sat up straight. He had landed in a patch of blue-green grass, surrounded by a dense thicket of spruce trees. His right leg stretched out before him, his swollen ankle looking as battered as the Elytra wings dangling from a nearby branch.

Mason wiggled his toes, grateful to see that they still worked. But when he tried to straighten his leg, pain shot through his ankle. *It's sprained,* he realized. *Or maybe even broken. And I'm alone in the woods!.*

Squawk! The parrot hopped closer, pecking through the grass as if looking for its dinner.

"Okay, so I'm not alone," said Mason, his voice wobbly. "But I might as well be."

The bird responded by flapping its wings—and taking flight.

"No, Hiss! Come back! I didn't mean that!" Mason watched as the bird fluttered away, disappearing in the maze of branches above.

"*Now* I'm alone," he said in the tiniest voice. His stomach squeezed.

He thought of Luna and Asher, miles away on the wrecked ship. *What would Luna do?* he wondered.

Check your supplies. He could hear her voice in his head, clear as a bell.

He still wore his trident at his waist. The weapon looked scratched and slightly bent. "But it's a weapon all the same," he said out loud, to any mobs lurking in the trees surrounding him. In his canvas sack, he had three or four firework rockets, but no flint and steel. And a potion of leaping.

At the thought of leaping, Mason winced. He rubbed his ankle, which was turning purplish-gray. *Should I call for help?* he wondered. *Would anyone hear?*

His mind flashed on a memory—the last thing he could picture before he had crashed into the trees. There was a campfire, back on the rocky beach. He could picture the logs so clearly, perfectly placed the way Asher would have arranged them. *Someone built that fire,* he decided. *Which means someone is nearby. Can I get to them?*

He pushed himself to standing, using his trident like a crutch. But after one step, his ankle buckled beneath him. "Uff!" He gripped his trident, trying to pull himself up again, but it was no use.

As Mason sank back down, he stared at his bent trident. Would the riptide enchantment still work? Could he launch himself out of the woods? If only it would rain!

He checked the sky. Through the dense branches overhead, the late afternoon sunlight trickled down. Any other day, he'd welcome that warmth and light. But today, he squeezed his eyes shut—blocking it out and keeping his hot tears at bay.

There was only one thing left to do. He cupped his hand to his mouth. "Help!" he cried.

"Help, help, help!" His voice bounced off the trees and echoed back at him.

Would anyone hear? Mason pictured the campfire again, which suddenly seemed very far away. He imagined Wither still flying through the air, miles away now with her Elytra wings.

She wouldn't help me anyway, he reminded himself. *Even after Asher and I tried to help her! Even after we flew all that way to find her wrecked ship!*

Mason leaned back with a sigh. *No one is going to help,* he decided. *I'm all alone.*

But the woods had suddenly grown noisy.

He heard the flutter of wings overhead, the breaking of twigs behind him, and then . . .

Hissss.

Mason's eyes blinked open. He grabbed his trident, just as the parrot landed on his shoulder.

"Hiss!" he scolded. "You have to stop sneaking up on me like that!"

"You should be thanking him." A girl's voice rang out from the trees. Mason whirled around just in time to see Wither stepping from the woods, her wings still strapped to her back.

Relief washed over Mason like rain, trailed by suspicion. "You followed me!"

She shrugged. "Hiss followed you," she said. "So I didn't really have a choice."

On an impulse, Mason reached for his Elytra wings, pulling them closer.

Wither's face hardened. "What? Do you really think I'd steal *those*?"

Mason looked again, noticing the jagged tear running down one wing. The other was frayed and bent. He let go, and then saw that Wither's wings were barely even scratched. "You didn't crash?" he asked.

She shook her head and smirked. "I cleared the trees. I figured I'd learn from your mistakes." When she saw his ankle, she sucked in her breath. "What happened?"

Mason touched his swollen skin. "It's sprained, or maybe broken. I was trying to get to the campfire, but . . . I don't think I can walk."

"Campfire?"

"The one on the beach. Someone started a fire there. Didn't you see it?"

Hope flickered in Wither's eyes, brighter than the flames of the campfire. "Who started it?"

Mason shrugged. "I don't know."

"My parents," she whispered, staring off into the distance. "Which way? Show me where you saw the fire!"

Mason pointed weakly back over the trees.

As Wither turned, he thought for a moment that she was going to take off running. *She's going to leave me here, with a sprained ankle!*

But she didn't. Wither hesitated, as if torn. Then she sighed deeply and began untangling Mason's wings from the trees.

"What are you doing?" he asked.

"Making a sled," she said. "If you can't walk, I'm going to have to pull you."

He sat in disbelief, watching as she tied a lead rope to the wings.

"Climb on," she said. "And hurry—I don't have all day."

Mason rolled onto the wings more than climbed. As Wither began to pull, grunting with each step, Mason felt the ground slip away beneath him.

Something else did, too. His suspicions—the ones

that had kept him wary of Wither and her brother—began to fall away. *She's helping me,* he realized. *She's actually helping me! So she can't be a griefer.*

As the trees thinned, Mason searched the sky for a trail of smoke, for any sign of the campfire. Now that he knew Wither was telling the truth, he wanted to help her, too.

All she wants is to find her parents, he reminded himself. *Maybe they drowned in the stormy sea. But . . .* He felt a familiar rush of hope. *Maybe they didn't.*

CHAPTER 14

As the sky darkened, Wither began to pull faster, tugging on the "sled" beneath Mason. "You're so heavy!" she said, panting. "Lie down or something, will you?"

He tried lying back, but it gave him the willies. Any moment now, hostile mobs could spawn. *And they'll catch me snoozing,* he realized, keeping his trident close at hand.

"Where's the campfire?" Wither asked again, an accusatory tone in her voice. "You said it was near the beach!"

Mason sat back up. "It was!" He scanned the rocky shore ahead, searching for a flicker of light or the glow of embers. He saw nothing but a few stars twinkling in the sky.

"Well it's not here now," said Wither. She let go of the rope, letting Mason's winged sled slide to a stop. Then she started jogging across the shore toward the water.

"Wait!" Mason cried. He wanted to run after her, but his ankle felt so swollen, it was no use. Instead, he kept watch for mobs, glancing over his shoulder every few seconds.

When Wither disappeared in the darkness, his stomach tightened. Then he heard a shout.

"I found it!" she cried. "I found the fire pit!" She raced back into view. "Mom! Dad! Are you here?" She scanned the ground, as if searching for footprints.

Mason wanted to shush her—to remind her that it was dark, and they needed to hide or find shelter before mobs spawned. But then he remembered his own first days without Uncle Bart. *I would be hollering for him now, too,* he realized. *If I thought he was still alive.*

So while Wither called into the night, he tilted his head, listening for a response.

Hissss.

"Quiet!" he scolded the parrot. "I'm trying to hear."

But the hissing behind him grew louder.

When Mason finally turned, his heart lurched. Hiss the Parrot was nowhere in sight. Instead, a hissing green mob crept out from behind a bush.

The creeper was mere feet away. Any moment now, it would blow.

Mason grabbed his trident and wound back his arm. Could he launch the trident from where he sat on the ground?

"Don't!" shouted Wither. "It'll explode!"

Mason fell backward as she yanked the wings

beneath him. He heard her panting as she pulled him away from the creeper, toward safety. And just in time.

Boom!

The creeper exploded, showering Mason with gunpowder. He wiped his face clean and blew out his breath. Then he whispered weakly, "Thanks. I thought it was Hiss!"

Wither nodded solemnly. "Me, too. But we were wrong. *Way* wrong."

Mason stared at the pile of gunpowder where the hissing creeper had stood. *I was wrong about a lot of things,* he decided. *The hissing parrot turned out to be a creeper. The good-for-nothing griefer turned out to be a . . . friend.*

"Thanks, Wither," he said again, when he could finally catch his breath. *Wither?* He clapped his hand over his mouth. Had he just said her nickname out loud?

"Huh?" She furrowed her brow.

"What I meant was, um . . ." Mason stammered. Finally, he just held out his hand. "I'm Mason."

She hesitated, but finally reached out to shake his hand. "I'm Savannah," she said. "And my brother back at the ship is Chase, just in case you got his name wrong, too." She grinned.

Mason cleared his throat. "Alright, well, we'd better find some shelter."

Savannah shook her head. "My parents are close by. I can feel it! And I think I saw footprints." She pulled a torch out of her sack and used the flint and steel to light it. "C'mon," she said.

"Um, I can't," said Mason. He pointed toward his ankle.

Savannah blew out an exasperated sigh.

"Just go without me," he said. "Let's relight the campfire and I'll stand guard on the beach."

A smile twitched at the corner of her mouth. "You mean 'sit guard'?"

He rolled his eyes. "Just give me something to light the fire with."

She pulled him closer to the burned-out fire pit, and then relit the logs. "The flames should keep mobs away," she said. "As long as you stay close to them."

"Where am I going to go?" joked Mason.

But as Savannah turned and headed off into darkness, the smile left his face. He'd never, ever before felt quite so alone.

As the logs crackled beside him and waves lapped against shore, he wanted to sleep. He wanted to close his eyes and wake up back in the underwater village, with his brother safely by his side. But home suddenly felt very far away.

And Asher is still stuck on a shipwreck in the middle of the ocean, he realized, his stomach knotting up all over again.

He had just begun to drift off when he heard Asher calling to him. "Wake up!" he was saying. "Wake up!"

Mason's eyelids flew open. Stars twinkled overhead, and his brother was nowhere in sight. *Just a dream,* he realized sadly, sinking back down onto the ground.

"Wake up!" Savannah shouted.

Mason jumped up, forgetting his sprained ankle. Forgetting the pain.

She was sprinting toward him, an army of groaning mobs staggering behind her. *Zombies!* Mason realized with a start. But why wasn't she fighting them?

As his eyes fell again on the monsters, he saw a trident sticking out from a green mob's thigh, wobbling with each step. Savannah *had* fought, but she'd lost her weapon.

She stared at him with wild eyes, as if willing him to do something. He pulled his own weapon, bracing himself for a fight. *A one-legged fight,* he thought as he wobbled on his ankle.

But as Savannah raced toward him, she shook her head. "There's too many. Just get to the water!"

She threw her arm under his and helped him limp toward the waves. Every step shot waves of pain up through his ankle and leg. But the zombies were so close now, Mason could hear them growling, could feel their hot, putrid breath on the back of his neck.

The first step into the cool water numbed his ankle. He sank downward, low enough so that he could swim in the surf rather than run. Then he spun around, wondering if the zombies had followed.

Some of the undead mobs stayed on shore, pacing and grunting in frustration. But others staggered forward into the waves. Savannah started to back up, pulling Mason with her into deeper water.

"Take this!" he cried, giving her his trident.

With the weapon in her hand, Savannah's face

hardened. She stepped forward, charging the nearest zombie. *Thwack! Thwack, thwack!* She knocked it off balance.

Thwack, thwack, thwack! The next zombie fell.

When Savannah dove underwater after it, Mason's mouth went dry. "What are you doing?" he cried, his voice cracking.

There she was! Coming back up now, with her own trident in her hand. She'd pulled it from the leg of the fallen mob, Mason realized. As she tossed his own weapon back toward him in the choppy waves, she held up her glowing trident.

With the sharp, enchanted weapon, she battled the next beast till it fell with a grunt and a splash. And then the next. *She's like Asher,* Mason realized. *She won't quit until the last mob falls.*

And finally, it did.

Savannah spun around, searching the waves for any last mobs—for a mottled green arm to rise from the waves to challenge her. Then she heaved a great sigh and sunk into the water beside Mason. As she caught her breath, Mason saw her look back toward the line of trees.

"Did you find your parents?" he asked.

She shook her head. When her lip began to quiver, she turned away. She dove low into the waves and then rolled onto her back, staring at the stars above.

What can I say? Mason wondered. *What can I do?*

When he glanced again at Savannah, he saw the water near her began to foam. It churned and swelled, as if any moment now, the tide would begin to roll *out* to sea instead of in toward shore. He rubbed his eyes. What was he was seeing?

When the zombie rose from the water, Mason's stomach dropped. *She didn't get them all!* he realized. *There's one left!*

But in the moonlight, he saw that this wasn't a zombie at all. Its skin was pale blue, not green. And it wore tattered brown robes instead of blue.

A drowned! Mason wanted to cry out. *One of the zombies we fought turned into a drowned!*

But Mason's voice caught in his throat.

Because the beast was inches away from Savannah. And it held a trident of its own.

CHAPTER 15

The drowned locked eyes with Mason. It let out an eerie growl. And then it stepped forward toward Savannah.

Without another thought, Mason sprang into action. He wound back his arm and launched his trident. *Whack!* It struck the drowned in the chest.

Mason felt his own body lurch forward with the weapon, carried by the riptide enchantment. He landed in the waves inches from the drowned, blocking Savannah's body with his own.

He was close enough now to look straight into the mob's gaping, glowing eyes. Close enough to yank the trident from its chest and strike it again.

But the drowned fought back. It growled with rage and swung its weapon.

Mason raised his trident to block the blow. *Clash!* Metal struck metal, and pain rippled through Mason's shoulder.

When the drowned lowered its weapon, Mason tried to strike again. But his shoulder throbbed. He barely grazed the mottled flesh of the drowned.

With an angry grunt, it lunged.

"No!" Savannah shouted from behind.

Thwack!

The arrow came from out of nowhere. Mason watched, as if in slow motion, as it struck the drowned in the forehead. Had Savannah found a bow?

He whirled around. But Savannah held only a trident, and she was looking backward, too.

Someone was on the beach, sprinting toward the water. A man with a beard . . . and a bow. "Savannah!" he cried.

He knows her! Mason realized. He watched his friend's expression change from shock to relief and then . . . joy.

She rushed out of the water, tripping once and then pushing herself back up to her feet. As she sprinted toward the man, Mason heard her shout, "Daddy!"

A woman had emerged from the woods now, too. As she hurried across the beach, Mason heard her crying out for Savannah.

His knees suddenly buckled, and he sank back down into the water. *We found them,* he realized. *We found Wither's parents—no, we found* Savannah's *parents. And they survived!*

Memories flooded his mind of everything that had happened in the last few hours. The flight. The crash. The sprained ankle. The zombies. And the drowned.

Her parents survived, he thought again. *And somehow, so did we.*

* * *

"Thank you," Savannah's mother said again.

They were sitting by the campfire, roasting salmon filets, as the sun rose in the eastern sky. "For what?" Mason asked.

"For saving our daughter from the drowned."

Mason fought the urge to laugh out loud. "I didn't save her!" he said. "She saved me. When I hurt my ankle, I mean. She pulled me out of the woods."

Savannah shrugged. "You did kind of save me from that drowned. So, I guess we saved each other." She shot him a smile, warm as the morning sunshine.

"Now we just need someone to save us from this island." Her father's gruff voice rang out across the beach, from where he stood watch near the water. "Do you see many ships out here?" he asked Mason.

A lump formed in Mason's throat. He shook his head no. "Your ship was the only one I've seen since . . . well, since my uncle's." *Only two ships in all those months,* he realized. *And both wrecked at sea.*

"But you have a rowboat!" he suddenly remembered. "Savannah said you were in a boat when the storm blew in."

Her mother sighed. "It was destroyed by the time we washed up on this island," she said. "We're using it for firewood right now." She gestured toward the campfire.

"Mason has a rowboat, back at our ship," said Savannah. She glanced at Mason, and then her eyes fell, resting on her hands in her lap.

Is she feeling guilty for almost stealing it? he wondered. That night seemed so long ago. And now he understood why she had wanted the boat so badly. *She'd wanted to find her parents. And somehow, she did!*

When he felt Savannah's parents' eyes on him, he nodded. "Our boat is solid," he said. "If we can get back to the ship, we can take the rowboat back to the mainland."

Savannah's father plunked down on the nearest log. "*If* we can get back to the ship," he said. "If we could do that, we would have done it days ago." He studied the horizon, as if hoping again that a ship with a white, billowy sail would appear.

"What about your wings?" Mason asked Savannah. "Mine were shredded to pieces when I crashed, but yours are still good."

"You want me to fly alone, you mean?" A shadow of doubt crossed her face. Or maybe even fear.

Mason blinked. *That's why she wanted Asher to fly with her!* he suddenly realized. *She wanted his firework rockets. But she was also afraid to fly alone.*

He scooted closer to Savannah in the sand. "You can do it," he said. "I have firework rockets." As he pointed toward his sack, his remembered something else. "And I have potion of leaping!"

She licked her lips nervously.

Savannah's mother reached over and squeezed her

daughter's hand. "You don't have to," she said reassuringly. "Not if you don't want to."

Savannah took a deep breath. "I *do* have to," she said. "Because this guy here isn't going to be able to get off the ground." She gestured toward Mason's ankle. "I mean, I pretty much have to do everything around here." She rolled her eyes in jest.

She's back! Mason realized with a grin. *And she's going to do it. She's going to fly for help.* For the first time in a very long time, he felt a rush of hope.

After a salmon breakfast, Savannah slid on her wings. Her mother tightened them around her waist and then turned quickly, as if she were about to cry.

"She's really good at flying," said Mason. "You'll see." Worry niggled at him, too, but he forced a smile. Then he crawled through the sand toward his canvas sack. "Here are the rockets," he said, handing them to Savannah's dad. "When she's ready, we'll light one."

Savannah's dad nodded and reached for his flint and steel.

"Wait!" Mason remembered. "Drink this first, Savannah."

When he handed her the potion, she wrinkled her nose.

Mason chuckled. "Don't worry. I mean, potion of leaping doesn't taste great," he said, "but I've had worse."

Savannah held her nose as she took a quick swig. Immediately, she sprang forward, trying out her bouncy legs. "Whoa!" she cried. "This stuff works!"

Mason nodded. "Don't waste it—it'll wear off quickly."

Savannah's dad gave his daughter a hug and then pulled out his flint and steel. When a flame sparked, he lit the fuse of Savannah's firework rocket and tucked two more rockets into her backpack.

When she turned toward Mason, he saw again the fear in her eyes. But he saw something else, too: determination. *Just like Asher,* he thought. *She's got her mind set on getting back to that ship, and she will.*

As the rocket flamed in her hand, Savannah began to leap, taking great strides toward the beach. Just before hitting water, she jumped skyward. Her wings—and the blazing firework rocket—did the rest.

Squawk!

Hiss appeared from out of nowhere. With a flap of his crimson wings, he took off after Savannah. In seconds, he was by her side.

"Yes!" cried Mason, pumping his fist.

Savannah was flying, but now she wouldn't be flying alone.

*   *   *

As the morning stretched into afternoon, Mason watched the water. Savannah's dad paced the shoreline, and her mother busied herself fishing.

When the rowboat finally came into view, Mason squinted, wondering if his eyes were playing tricks on him. Then he saw someone wave from the boat.

Whoever is in there is coming for us! he realized. He jumped up—bum ankle and all—and cheered.

As the boat rowed closer, he saw that it was full of people. Luna and Asher sat in front, and Savannah and her brother, Chase, in back. But another boat bobbed along behind.

Even from this distance, Mason recognized the woman rowing it, her long white hair rippling in the wind. Ms. Beacon had come, too, with enough room in her boat for them all!

Savannah's mother rushed into the waves, eager to greet the boats, just as one of the passengers dived overboard. Mason spotted his brother's green T-shirt and his red head bobbing in the water. "Asher!" he cried. "Be careful!"

A minute later, his brother jogged out of the waves, dripping from head to toe. As he got closer, a grin stretched across his freckled face. He dove low to give Mason a ginormous wet hug.

"Ew!" cried Mason, trying to shake it off. "Stop!"

But as Asher dropped into the sand beside him, Mason threw his arm around his little brother's shoulder. "We did it!" he said. "We helped them find their parents."

He suddenly felt someone standing over him in the sand. Chase dropped down beside Asher, and from the smile on Asher's face, Mason could tell that the boys had become friends.

Chase picked at a fingernail and then asked the question that seemed to have been on the tip of his tongue. "Why'd you help us?" he asked. "Me and Savannah. We weren't exactly nice to you."

Mason shrugged. "Because when our ship went down and we lost Uncle Bart, there was no one to help us," he said. "We wanted to help someone the way we wish someone had helped us."

Asher shook his head. "Someone *did* help us," he argued. Then he pointed. "We had Luna. And Ms. Beacon." He explained to Chase how Luna had taught them how to live underwater, and how the old woman had supplied them with powerful potions when they needed them most.

Mason glanced back at the surf, where Luna was helping Ms. Beacon out of her rowboat. He nodded. "That's true," he said to Asher. "We did have help."

"Even though you didn't really want it at first," Asher pointed out.

Mason thought of the moment he had first met Luna, when he didn't trust her at all. He laughed out loud. "No, I didn't. And Ms. Beacon didn't trust us at first either. But somehow . . . we all helped each other."

"Maybe we can help you now, too," said Savannah.

Mason turned to find her squatting beside the campfire.

"Maybe we can help you find your uncle."

Mason started to shake his head. *Uncle Bart is gone,* he knew. But Savannah stared at him so intensely, he didn't want to argue. So instead, he just shrugged. "Maybe."

As he turned back toward the water, he saw Hiss

land on Luna's shoulder. And a thought fluttered through his mind.

If parrots can hiss like creepers and griefers can become friends, maybe long-lost uncles can *be found,* he decided. *Who knows?*

He threw his arm around Asher and answered again. "Maybe."